This book belongs to:

....

For Flora.

E.D.

For my brother, Mitch.

L.D.

ORCHARD BOOKS

First published in Great Britain in 2022 by Hodder & Stoughton

1 3 5 7 9 10 8 6 4 2

© Hachette Children's Group 2022
Illustrations by Liam Darcy

A CIP catalogue record for this book is available from the British Library.

UK ISBN 978 1 40836 7919
ANZ ISBN 978 1 40836 7902

Printed and bound in China

Orchard Books
An imprint of Hachette Children's Group
Part of Hodder & Stoughton
Carmelite House
50 Victoria Embankment
London EC4Y 0DZ

An Hachette UK Company
www.hachette.co.uk

www.hachettechildrens.co.uk

THE TWELVE DINOSAURS OF CHRISTMAS

Evie Day Liam Darcy

ORCHARD

On the first day of Christmas,
my grandpa gave to me . . .
a Santasaurus and her dino baby.

On the second day of Christmas,
my grandpa gave to me . . .
two merry raptors
and a Santasaurus
and her dino baby.

On the third day of Christmas,
my grandpa gave to me . . .
three troodon,
two merry raptors
and a Santasaurus
and her dino baby.

On the fourth day of Christmas,
my grandpa gave to me . . .
four jobaria,

three troodon,
two merry raptors
and a Santasaurus
and her dino baby.

On the fifth day of Christmas,
my grandpa gave to me . . .
five tinselled triceratops . . .

four jobaria,
three troodon,
two merry raptors
and a Santasaurus
and her dino baby.

On the sixth day of Christmas,
my grandpa gave to me . . .
six T-rexes wrapping,
five tinselled triceratops . . .
four jobaria,
three troodon,
two merry raptors
and a Santasaurus
and her dino baby.

On the seventh
day of Christmas,
my grandpa gave to me . . .
seven brontosauruses baking,

six T-rexes wrapping,

five tinselled triceratops . . .

four jobaria,

three troodon,

two merry raptors

and a Santasaurus

and her dino baby.

On the eighth day of Christmas,
my grandpa gave to me . . .
eight eoraptors eating,

seven brontosauruses baking,

six T-rexes wrapping,

five tinselled triceratops . . .

four jobaria,

three troodon,

two merry raptors

and a Santasaurus

and her dino baby.

On the ninth day of Christmas,
my grandpa gave to me . . .
nine spinosauruses sparkling,

eight eoraptors eating,
seven brontosauruses baking,
six T-rexes wrapping,
five tinselled triceratops . . .
four jobaria,
three troodon,
two merry raptors
and a Santasaurus
and her dino baby.

On the tenth day of Christmas,
my grandpa gave to me . . .
ten deinonychuses dashing,

nine spinosauruses sparkling,

eight eoraptors eating,

seven brontosauruses baking,

six T-rexes wrapping,

five tinselled triceratops . . .

four jobaria,

three troodon,

two merry raptors

and a Santasaurus

and her dino baby.

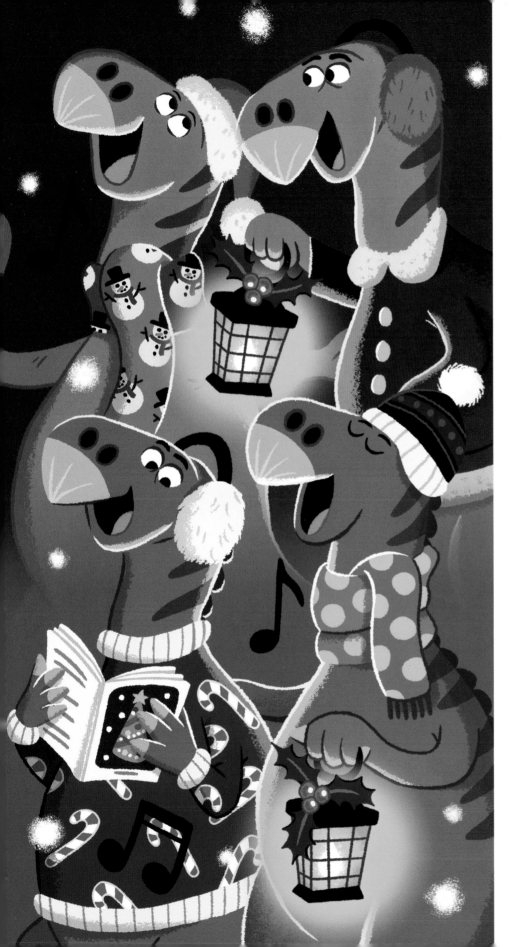

On the eleventh
day of Christmas,
my grandpa gave to me . . .
eleven iguanodons glowing,
ten deinonychuses dashing,
nine spinosauruses sparkling,
eight eoraptors eating,
seven brontosauruses baking,
six T-rexes wrapping,
five tinselled triceratops . . .
four jobaria,
three troodon,
two merry raptors
and a Santasaurus
and her dino baby.

On the twelfth day of Christmas,
my grandpa gave to me . . .
twelve pterodactyls twirling . . .

. . . eleven iguanodons glowing,
ten deinonychuses dashing,
nine spinosauruses sparkling,
eight eoraptors eating,
seven brontosauruses baking,
six T-rexes wrapping,
five tinselled triceratops . . .
four jobaria,
three troodon,
two merry raptors and
a Santasaurus and her . . .

How to sing along to The Twelve Dinosaurs of Christmas:

Twelve **tero-dac-tils** twirling,

eleven **ig-wana-dons** glowing,

ten **di-non-ee-cus-es** dashing,

nine **spine-o-saw-rus-es** sparkling,

eight **ee-o-rap-ters** eating,

seven **bron-toh-saw-rus-es** baking,

six **Tee-rex-es** wrapping,

five tinselled **tri-sera-tops** . . .

four **joh-bear-ee-ah**,

three **trow-a-don**,

two merry **rap-ters**

and a **Santa-saw-rus** and her **dino baby!**